Pick-A-Path®#5

The Super Trail Bike Race

by RICHARD WENK

illustrated by DAVID GOTHARD

SCHOLASTIC INC.
New York Toronto London Auckland Sydney

*To Francine Pascal, for her kindness, generosity,
invaluable assistance, and this job.*

*And to Michael Stewart for things too numerous
to mention*

R. W.

To Alan Jr.

D. G.

ISBN 0-590-32927-8

12 11 10 9 8 7 6 5 4   3 4 5 6 7/9

Printed in the U.S.A.   40

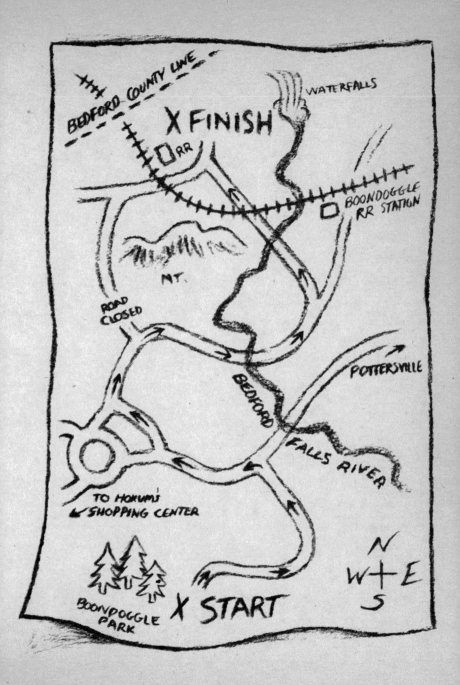

READ THIS FIRST!

Imagine a free shopping spree in the world's biggest department store. Imagine winning a whole recreation center for your town, with a swimming pool, tennis courts, and a video arcade. Hard to believe, right? Wrong.

Today is the "First and Last Annual Horace B. Hokum Bicycle Race." And those are the grand prizes. You could be the winner!

Start reading on page 1 and keep reading until you have to make a choice. Then decide what you want to do and turn to that page. Keep following the directions until you come to **THE END**.

If you don't like one ending, just go back and choose a different path. Every choice you make leads to a new story! It is all up to you!

Horace B. Hokum is the owner of Hokum's Department Store and is one of the richest men in the country. Last month Mr. Hokum decided to hold a one-time-only bicycle race for kids. The winner will get a free shopping spree in Hokum's Department Store, and his or her town will win a recreation center.

It's the morning of the race, and you're in the garage putting the finishing touches on your custom-made trail bike. The wheels have been oiled and perfectly balanced. The shiny red paint is trimmed in gold, and the handlebars have been padded.

You are checking your knapsack one last time when your best friend, Alana, rides up. She's in the race, too. She looks as nervous as you feel.

"Are you almost ready?" Alana asks.

"All set," you reply with a brave smile. Together you ride off toward the starting line in Boondoggle Park.

Turn to **page 2.**

A huge crowd has gathered to watch the start of the race. Twelve towns have entered, with two kids representing each town. You and Alana are the youngest. You notice that the Coleman twins from Pottersville are in the race. They're mean. And they cheat.

Everyone gets a map of the racecourse. Then Horace B. Hokum makes a surprise announcement.

"Welcome, racers. You will all start on your bicycles. But you may finish the race to the Bedford County line in any way you like, *except* by automobile. That is the only rule. Now, take your places, and may the most resourceful person win," he says.

You go to your spot on the starting line. The starter raises his pistol and—*bang!*— you're off!

Go on to the next page.

You may be the smallest, but you're also the quickest. You zoom off ahead of everyone else. The hometown crowd cheers you on as you round the corner in first place. Your legs pedal like there's no tomorrow, and after two miles you have a pretty good lead.

At the five-mile mark you look back and see that someone is gaining on you. It's the Coleman twins, on their bicycle built for two. They try to pass, but you start to pull away.

All of a sudden, one of the Colemans shoves a stick into the spokes of your front wheel. The bike stops short and sends you flying head over heels through the air. Luckily, you land unhurt on a pile of leaves. You can hear the Coleman twins laughing in the distance.

Turn to **page 4.**

Tears well up in your eyes as other racers pass you by. You look for your bike and find it crumpled by the side of the road. Two spokes are bent, and the front tire is flat.

You are about to give up when Alana pulls alongside you. "Hop on my handlebars," she says. "We'll win the race together."

But you're not sure if both of you on one bike can catch the others. Maybe you could fix your bike if you tried. You don't have much time to decide.

If you decide to ride off with Alana,
turn to **page 5.**

If you stay and try to fix your bike,
turn to **page 29.**

"It's a deal!" you exclaim. You jump onto Alana's handlebars, and off you go together.

After about two miles, you see that Alana can't pedal fast enough with the extra weight. The going is just too slow for you two to catch up to anyone.

"Pull over," you yell. "There's a better way than this!"

Alana skids to a halt, and you leap off the handlebars. It was a good idea to pack your knapsack—you pull out your trusty roller skates and a long elastic cord. You attach one end of the cord to your belt and the other to the back of the bicycle seat. Then you put on the skates.

"See? Now I'm on wheels, and all you have to do is pull me!"

"You're a genius," says Alana.

Turn to **page 6.**

6   Twenty minutes later you're back in the thick of the race. You glide in and around the other racers. Your idea is a smashing success.

But Alana is beginning to tire. Just then you start down a steep hill. You glide right past Alana, and now you are pulling her!

"Thanks for the lift!" shouts Alana.

"Anytime, pal," you reply.

Go on to the next page.

By the time you reach the bottom of the hill, Alana has caught her breath and is once again pedaling faster than anyone else. Within minutes the Coleman twins are in sight. It's just a matter of time now before you pass them.

Just then the Colemans make a sharp turn onto a side road. What could they be doing? That's not where the map says to go. Could it be a shortcut? It might be a trick.

Alana has seen them turn off, too. "What should we do? We can't let them get too far ahead," she yells back to you.

You have to make up your mind. You're going to reach the turn any second now.

*If you tell Alana to follow
the Coleman twins,
turn to* **page 8.**

*If you decide to stay on course,
turn to* **page 10.**

"Let's follow them," you yell to Alana. "They must know a shortcut."

"Okay, hold on!" Alana makes a sharp turn onto the narrow gravel road. At first you have a hard time staying on the roller skates and almost fall. But soon the road turns to pavement. Alana stops the bike.

"Are you thinking what I'm thinking?" she says. You are. Where are the Coleman twins? You were right behind them, but now, somehow, they've vanished.

Just then a voice bellows to you from a loudspeaker: "Stay right where you are! You are under arrest for trespassing on the property of Mr. Horace B. Hokum."

A pair of security guards leads you away. By the time you can explain, the Coleman twins are on their way to winning the race.

THE END

"I think it's a trick. Don't follow them!" you yell ahead to Alana.

Alana stays on course, and you slowly begin to pull away from the pack. After some time you agree to switch places with Alana, who is now very tired. You leap aboard the bike, and with Alana in tow, pedal off toward the finish line.

You're moving faster than you've ever gone before. Your legs and feet are just a blur as you round corner after corner.

There are only a few miles to go now, and you can taste victory. Just then, disaster strikes! Blocking the road ahead of you is a stalled freight train!

Go on to the next page.

You screech to a halt. Alana crashes into you from behind, and you both tumble to the ground.

After you help Alana to her feet, you look to see if there is a way around the train. But the cars snake their way down the tracks for what looks like miles. Just then the engineer walks by.

"How long will the train be here?" you ask.

"She'll be leaving for Bedford Falls in about five minutes," he replies.

Alana looks at you as if she has the same thought. If you wait for the train to move, the other riders will catch up. You could search for a way around, or…there are two open boxcars that no one is watching. You could climb aboard and be in Bedford Falls before anybody else.

If you look for a way around the train, turn to **page 13.**

If you climb aboard the train, turn to **page 20.**

You both decide that it's too dangerous to jump aboard the train. You've just got to find a way around it. You turn left and start to look for the end of the train. But you never get there.

About two hundred yards down the line, you run smack into the Bedford Falls River. You can't get around the train—it's stuck on the railroad bridge— and you can't cross the river.

You sit down on the bank and try to hold back the tears. You wanted very badly to win that recreation center for your town.

Just then Alana nudges you. "What's that?" she asks.

There, grounded on the bank of the river, is an abandoned wooden raft.

Turn to **page 14.**

14 You and Alana dash over to the raft. It looks creaky, but it's your only chance. Very carefully, you step onto the raft. So far so good. Then Alana hands you the bicycle. The raft is still floating! Alana steps aboard, too. It will work!

You push out into the current and float to the other side of the river. You maneuver the raft to shore and hop off. Mr. Hokum *did* say that the most resourceful person would win the race.

Go on to the next page.

With Alana riding on the handlebars, **15** you pedal toward the finish line. Then, with about two miles to go, you spot the Coleman twins up ahead of you. This is your chance to get even.

Your legs, moving like pistons, begin to pump faster and faster. In spite of the extra weight, you are catching up to the tired twins.

With a mile to go, you pull up even with them. It's going to come down to the wire. Suddenly, up ahead, you see it—a long ditch that must be at least three feet deep. The only way across it is a narrow plank. But you will have to cut in front of the twins in order to get to it. That could be dangerous. You've already seen their nasty tricks.

You could try to jump over the ditch, but with Alana on the handlebars it would be very risky.

Turn to **page 16.**

"Do you think you could hold on if I tried to jump over the ditch?" you ask Alana.

"I'm not sure," she says, holding the handlebars even tighter.

There's no more time to think. You must decide now!

If you risk a jump over the ditch,
turn to **page 19.**

If you try for the narrow plank,
turn to **page 38.**

You turn your bike around and start back. You've only gone about ten feet when you run over a sharp, pointed rock. Both tires flatten in seconds. You'll have to walk back to the main road and drag your bike with you. There is no way you can win the race now.

It seems like hours before you finally reach the main road. Your legs are sore and both feet have blisters. You slump down by the side of the road and wait for your family to come looking for you.

This is turning out to be the worst day of your life. You're just glad that it's almost...

THE END

"Hold on!" you yell to Alana. You push on the pedals as hard as you can and then pull the bike up with all your might. You close your eyes as the bike flies over the edge of the ditch. The wind rushes past your face.

You open your eyes as you land— *crunch!* The back tire lands safely by inches. Alana bounces up into the air, but never loses her grip. She hangs on as you fly past the cheering crowd and cross the finish line, the winners!

You can't believe it. The whole town swarms around you and Alana and lifts you onto their shoulders. This is the most exciting day of your life! And you bet nobody thought the youngest racers would stand a chance.

THE END

20   As the engineer walks up and down on the other side of the train, you and Alana hide her bike and your roller skates in the bushes nearby.

"Okay, let's go," you whisper in a hurry.

Go on to the next page.

You boost yourselves up into an empty boxcar. You hunch down between two crates, and in a few minutes the train begins to move.

What a break, you think, as the train heads toward Bedford Falls. In a moment's time you and Alana will be crossing the finish line well ahead of the others. But suddenly the train speeds up. It reaches the Bedford Falls station and rumbles right through. There's no chance for you to get off!

"What will we do now?" cries Alana.

"We'll have to jump when the train slows down," you reply.

A minute later, as the train slows to round a bend, you grab Alana's hand, close your eyes, and jump. You both fall to the ground unhurt. But when you look around for a familiar sight, you can't find a single one. You're lost!

Turn to **page 22.**

You and Alana begin to wander about, looking for a house or a phone, so you can call for help. It's getting dark, and a light rain has begun to fall. All hope of winning the race has vanished. All you want to do now is get home.

Suddenly it begins to thunder and lightning. The sky is pitch black. The two of you dash through an open field, frantically looking for cover. Then, in the distance, you spot an old house standing alone on a hill.

You race up onto the porch, out of the rain. The house is completely dark. "It doesn't look like anyone lives here," you say. Alana rings the doorbell, but there is no answer.

"Should we go in?" asks Alana.

"I don't know. I will if you will," you
reply.

"I think we should. There might be a
phone inside," she says.

Turn to **page 24.**

24   Slowly you step toward the door. But before you can touch the doorknob, the door opens by itself! You look at Alana. She looks at you...you're both scared, but you enter the spooky mansion.

Inside, the furniture is covered with sheets, and there are cobwebs everywhere. You reach the bottom of a gigantic staircase, when all of a sudden there is a crack of thunder and a flash of lightning that reveals a terrible shadow on the stairs. You both scream at the top of your lungs!

If you remain in the house,
go on to the next page.

If you race out of the house
and into the night,
*turn to **page 44**.*

You're more frightened than you've ever been—and so is Alana. But you remind yourselves that you don't believe in ghosts. And the storm is blowing wildly now. So you stay inside the house searching each room for a telephone, but with no luck.

Finally there is only one more place to check—the attic. Slowly you push open the trap door.

Turn to **page 26.**

26   A flash of lightning floods the attic floor. And there, in the center of the room, is a small suitcase. You make your way through the dark and open the suitcase as the lightning flashes again. You can't believe your eyes! Inside, glistening brightly, is a pile of gold coins!

You switch on your flashlight to get a better look, and you see a note:

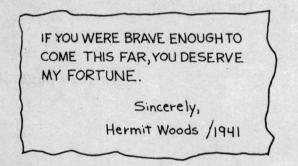

IF YOU WERE BRAVE ENOUGH TO COME THIS FAR, YOU DESERVE MY FORTUNE.

Sincerely,
Hermit Woods /1941

"We're rich!" screams Alana.

You'll be able to buy *two* recreation centers. All you have to do now is find your way home....

THE END

You stretch as far as you can and then lunge for the branch. For a second you think it will hold. But it doesn't. Your weight was too much. You begin to fall to the ground. You seem to be going in slow motion, just like in a dream.

You only hope you *are* dreaming now, because if you're not this may be...

THE END

"You better go without me," you say. "You might be our only chance to win."

Reluctantly Alana pedals off. You turn your attention to your bicycle. From your knapsack you pull out a spoke wrench and a small bicycle pump.

After removing the bent spokes, you try to inflate the tire. But the puncture is too big, and the tire stays flat. With nothing to patch the hole all looks lost. Then you get a brilliant idea. You'll use the gum you're chewing to plug the leak!

Quickly you stuff a small piece of your gum over the hole and fill the tire with air. It works! The patch holds! You leap on your bike and race off. You know you've got a lot of ground to make up.

Turn to **page 30.**

30   You pedal as hard and as fast as you can. Soon you're going faster than you've ever thought you could. You speed down hills and around corners. Somehow you will win this race and get even with those Coleman twins.

But at the twenty-mile mark you realize that you're not moving up fast enough. You've only passed four racers. It looks like the time you lost fixing your bike might be too much for you to overcome.

Just then you come to a fork in the road. The road on the left is closed. Your map says to take the one on the right. But the road that's closed just might be a shortcut. This could be the break you need. It could also lead to disaster. Should you take a chance?

If you take the closed road,
turn to **page 31.**

If you decide to play it safe and stay
on the open road, turn to **page 33.**

A shortcut could be your only chance. **31**
You've got to risk it. You cross your
fingers and start down the deserted dirt
road.

At first the going is smooth and swift.
At this pace you'll be back in the race in
no time. Then, without warning, the
road becomes bumpy and uneven.
Large rocks and deep ditches are
everywhere. You guide your way slowly
around these obstacles, but you're
losing valuable time.

Turn to **page 32.**

32   Suddenly the chewing-gum patch gives way, and the front tire begins to lose air. Soon the tire will be completely flat, and you'll be stranded in the middle of nowhere. And you're out of gum.

You could keep going on the dirt road and hope you don't get lost, or you could start back the way you came and look for help. But if you go back, will you still have a chance to win the race?

If you continue on,
turn to **page 35.**

If you decide to turn around
and go back,
turn to **page 17.**

You still think you have the time and the stamina to catch up and win the race. You tear off down the open road.

Without fear, you whiz along at incredible speed. Suddenly, out of nowhere, a squirrel scampers into the middle of the road, right in front of your bike. You're startled, but you react with catlike reflexes. Instantly you turn to the left and ride around the frightened animal. Whew! That was close.

Soon you begin to pass other racers. You've made it into seventh place. A few minutes later you pull alongside of Alana. She's glad to see you, but her report is not encouraging.

"We'll never catch the Coleman twins in time," says Alana. "They're too far ahead."

It looks like you will have to come up with a new plan. Just then a train whistle blows.

"I've got it!" you cry. "Follow me."

Turn to **page 34.**

34   With Alana by your side, you turn off into a side road, and within minutes you arrive at the Boondoggle railroad station. A long freight train sits motionless on the tracks.

"Why did you bring us here?" asks Alana.

"Because that train is going to take us to Bedford Falls," you answer with a grin. "We'll have to lock up our bikes and come back for them later after the race."

Turn to **page 21.**

You keep riding down the dirt road
hoping that help will appear around the
next turn. But it doesn't, and the tire is
almost flat now. It looks as if you made
the wrong decision.

You're about to give up all hope, when
suddenly you come upon an old, run-
down gas station. A man comes out of
the garage and looks at you suspiciously.
"You're the first person I've seen here in
years," he says. "What do you want?"

Turn to **page 36.**

"My tire is flat and I would like to have it fixed, please," you say.

The man smiles. "Why didn't you say so? We'll have that tire fixed in a jiffy!"

This is the best thing to happen all day. There is still time for you to win the race.

While the man repairs your tire you tell him about the race and the big prize. He tells you that his name is George Bailey. Ten years ago, the government decided to build a new road rather than repair this one. He couldn't afford to move, so he stayed. You ask him if this road is shorter than the new one.

"Depends," he mumbles. "It's half the distance but twice as rough."

Go on to the next page.

Minutes later the tire is patched, and you're all set to go. You thank Mr. Bailey and are about to race off when he says, "Wait a minute. If you want to save time, take the secret path behind the garage. You'll come to a hill, and just on the other side is the county line." He turns and disappears into the gas station.

You're not sure if you believe him or not. He is a little strange. But the road you were on *is* treacherous. You don't have much time to decide. Every minute counts.

If you take the secret path,
turn to **page 39.**

If you stay on the dirt road,
turn to **page 41.**

You steer the bicycle sharply to the right and swing in front of the Coleman twins. You look back just as one of them is about to grab the back of your bike. He's going to try to knock you into the ditch.

With all the strength you have left, you blast forward. He misses your bike by an inch. The Colemans lose their balance and fall into the muddy ditch.

You glide safely over the plank and cross the finish line. You are the winners! Later, Mr. Hokum announces that you will *both* get shopping sprees. Having a friend like Alana to share this with makes it twice as much fun!

THE END

Old Mr. Bailey may be a bit strange, but he did fix your tire for free. The other road is rough, and if it gets any rougher your bike might not make it. So you ride around to the rear of the station. You spot the path right away. It's just wide enough for you and your bicycle.

At first the woods are thick and the going is slow. Just when you think that you've made a mistake, the path widens and you begin to pick up speed.

You've been riding now for twenty minutes. A look at your watch tells you that if you don't come to that hill soon, you won't have a chance.

You tear around the final bend and reach the end of the path. What you see is not a hill but a towering mountain! You can't believe it. The finish line is just on the other side. The question is: How will you get there?

Turn to **page 40.**

40   You check your watch. If you can get over and down the mountain fast, you can still win. Just then you notice there is an entrance to an abandoned mine shaft at the base of the mountain. A sign nailed across it says DANGER. It's possible that the tunnel could run right through to the other side. Then again, it might not. If you got trapped, no one would ever find you. You think you can climb the mountain in time, but you've never climbed that high before. It's a risk either way.

*If you think you can climb
the mountain in time,
turn to* **page 42.**

*If you decide to enter the mine shaft,
turn to* **page 54.**

You decide to keep going on the rocky dirt road. At first the going is very slow. You'll never win at this rate. You decide to risk everything. Like a Hollywood stunt driver, you attack the jutting rocks and plunging ditches. The tire patch holds, and soon you're back on smooth ground. Nothing can stop you now!

THE END

P.S. If you want to know how the race ends, circle the first and the twentieth words on this page.

You hate to leave your bike behind, but there's no turning back now, so you leave it on the side of the path. You take a deep breath and then start to climb. At first the climbing is easy. There are lots of branches and rocks to hold on to. Inch by inch, foot by foot, you make your way up the mountain. Even though you're scared, you push on.

The minutes tick by as you move closer to the top. With only three feet to go, you pause on a narrow ledge to catch your breath. Suddenly, a huge bird swoops down out of the sky, missing you by inches! A moment later it attacks you again. You duck your head just in time. Then you see what's wrong—next to

you, on the ledge, is a nest with a baby bird in it. The mother wants you off that ledge.

You search frantically for something to hold on to. The only thing in sight is a small branch. Is it strong enough? Your only other chance is to make a jump for the top of the mountain, but you're not sure you can make it. And the bird is heading for you again. You have to decide now!

If you grab hold of the branch,
turn to **page 28.**

If you leap for the top,
turn to **page 45.**

43

44   You and Alana rush from the house as fast as your feet will take you. The thunder and lightning are nothing compared to the scare you just received.

It's raining so hard you can barely see. "Which way?"groans Alana.

"Anywhere but near that house!" you call back.

Soon you come to a road. Without slowing down a bit, you head for some flickering lights in the distance. As you get closer you see that it's the finish line! What luck!

You and Alana cross the line at the same time and are surrounded by the race officials. Then comes the shock of your life. You are the first ones to cross the finish line! Nobody else braved the storm. You're co-winners!

Not only will your town get the recreation center, but you both get to go on the shopping spree. And four hands are better than two!

THE END

You crouch down as low as you can, **45**
and just as the bird reaches you, you
leap with all your might. You stretch
your arms out as far as they will go. You
feel your fingers grip solid rock, and in
one swift motion you pull yourself up to
safety on the top of the mountain.

Scrambling to your feet, you dash
down through the trees on the other
side. Now you can see the finish line be-
low you. But your heart sinks. You don't
see a way to get down.

Turn to **page 47.**

You keep looking around until you discover a Park Ranger lookout tower not far off. You shout to the ranger inside.

"Excuse me. How do you get down from here?" The ranger looks a little startled. He asks you how you got *up* here. You quickly tell him and then explain why you must get to the bottom right away.

"There are only two ways down," he informs you. "Our weather balloon or Ol' Pete, my horse."

Neither of those sounds very fast. The horse looks old and tired, and a balloon only goes as fast as the wind. But you must pick one or the other.

If you ride the horse,
turn to **page 48.**

If you try the balloon,
turn to **page 51.**

You're up as high as you want to get right now, so you decide to gamble on the horse. The ranger helps you up onto Ol' Pete and hands you the reins.

"Don't expect too much. Pete hasn't gone faster than a trot in fifteen years," says the ranger. Well, it's better than walking. "Giddap!" you yell, and Ol' Pete begins his walk down the mountain.

Halfway to the bottom you see the Coleman twins in the distance. They're only minutes from the finish line. You plead with Ol' Pete to go faster, but he only slows down. It's just about over now. You gave it your best shot. And so did Ol' Pete.

"Well, you tried, Pete," you say to the lazy horse. "When we get to the finish line, I'll give you a carrot."

That's the magic word! *Carrot*! Like a bullet, Ol' Pete speeds down the mountain. Everything is a blur as you race to

the bottom and toward the finish line. **49**
It's all you can do to hold on as Ol' Pete
closes in on the Coleman twins. It's
going to be close.

Turn to **page 58.**

50   Without thinking, you try to leap over the widening gap. For a split second it looks as if you made it. But the ground you land on gives way. You fall backward into the black pit. . . .

You awake on top of a pile of mud and leaves. It must have broken your fall and saved your life. Next to you is your flashlight. It still works! You begin to search for a way out, but your chances are pretty slim.

During your search you discover a small cave. Inside, you find old pistols and swords scattered about. *What are they doing here?* you wonder.

Then you feel something under your foot. You brush aside the dirt to uncover an old map. You look closer. It's a treasure map! And it shows that the treasure is buried in the most incredible place—right behind your house! You'll be rich!

Now all you have to do is find your way out.

THE END

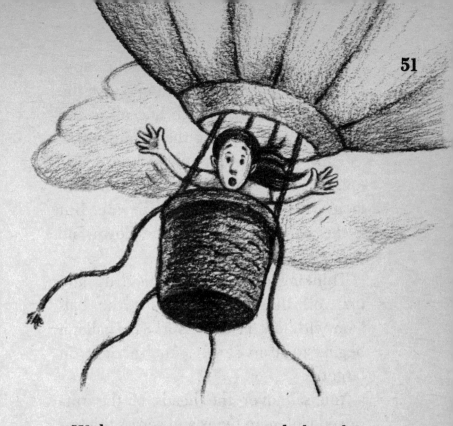

With no time to spare, you dash to the big hot-air balloon and leap into the basket. The ranger will go with you to guide it in the right direction. But just before he can get in, the ropes holding down the balloon give way, and you sail helplessly up into the air.

"What should I do?" you cry.

Turn to **page 52.**

You are too high up to hear the ranger's reply. You peer over the edge of the basket and see the finish line off in the distance. You're going the wrong way!

Things look bleak until, without warning, the wind changes and sends the balloon drifting toward the finish line. But if the balloon doesn't come down, no one will see you.

Thinking quickly, you reach up and turn off the flame that fills the balloon with air. That does it! The balloon begins to drop slowly. You're right on target.

You sail over the heads of the surprised Coleman twins and across the finish line. You're the winner! The balloon lands softly on the ground. No one will ever forget this exciting finish. You'll be a legend in Bedford County forever!

THE END

54   You take your flashlight from your knapsack and step into the dark, eerie mine. The deeper you go, the more worried you get. Each beam looks as if it's going to give way any second. The next step you take could be your last.

The narrow tunnel you've been walking in widens as you reach the center of the mine. Old-time miners' tools are scattered around the ground. Facing you are the entrances to four tunnels. Each tunnel goes in a different direction. You'll have to pick one of them.

Go on to the next page.

You are about to make your decision when, all of a sudden, you hear something. At first it's just a tiny creak. But then it gets louder. You feel dirt trickle onto your head. Then all at once the entire mine begins to quake.

Beams fall from everywhere, and the walls around you start to crumble. You look behind you and see that the ground is splitting apart! In a few seconds the entrance you came from will be blocked forever.

You've got to make a quick decision. You might be able to leap across the splitting floor and make it to safety. Or you could dash into one of the four tunnels and hope that it is the way out. One thing is for sure—if you stay where you are now you'll be buried alive.

*If you run to one of the tunnels,
turn to* **page 56.**

*If you try to get out of the mine,
turn to* **page 50.**

56   You run into the tunnel right in front of you. The falling rocks and heavy beams miss you by inches. There is no turning back now.

A little way in, you find an old mining car still on its tracks. Maybe these tracks will take you to an opening. You kick away the stones that are blocking the wheels and hop into the rolling car. It moves slowly along the rusty tracks. Then you come to a steep hill, and suddenly you are whizzing along in the dark. The only thing to fear now is a dead end.

Then, up ahead, you see a tiny speck of light. As you get closer you see that it's an exit. You made it through the mountain! You look for the brake on the mining car, but there isn't one! You can't stop!

Go on to the next page.

The car is still gaining speed when it reaches the exit. It flies from its tracks and continues across the ground and onto the road. Incredibly, you're heading right for the finish line! You're just a blur as you pass the Coleman twins, who are so surprised they fall off their bicycle. You rumble across the finish line, the winner!

Your town will get its recreation center, and you will get the shopping spree. Now all you have to do is figure out how to stop this thing!

THE END

58   The crowd is on its feet cheering this fantastic finish. With ten yards to go, you're neck and neck with the Colemans. In a final burst of speed, Ol' Pete explodes past the twins, and you win by a nose! Nobody can believe it. Your entire town is chanting your name. You are a hero!

Someone helps you off the horse and leads you to the grandstand. Reporters take your picture, and Horace B. Hokum awards you the key to his store. Then you remember your promise to Ol' Pete. You dash to the refreshment booth and come back with carrots in hand.

"I couldn't have done it without ya," you tell Ol' Pete. Somehow you know he understands.

THE END